BY
HIS
DESIRE

Kate Grey

Copyright © 2012 by Kate Grey.

All rights reserved. No part of this publication may be reproduced, distributed or transmitted in any form or by any means, including photocopying, recording, or other electronic or mechanical methods, without the prior written permission of the publisher, except in the case of brief quotations embodied in critical reviews and certain other noncommercial uses permitted by copyright law.

This is a work of fiction. Names, characters, places, and incidents are a product of the author's imagination. Locales and public names are sometimes used for atmospheric purposes. Any resemblance to actual people, living or dead, or to businesses, companies, events, institutions, or locales is completely coincidental.

Book Layout ©2013 BookDesignTemplates.com

By His Desire/ Kate Grey. -- 1st ed.
ISBN 978-1-4953767-1-9

CHAPTER 1

"Can I make a comment that will probably piss you off?"

Keith Logan glanced at his assistant, Valerie. "Nothing's ever stopped you before."

"Yeah, but I usually rip you about work-related stuff, and this is personal."

Keith turned back to the million dollar painting he'd just lent to the Modern Art Museum. "Go for it," he said, knowing she would anyway.

"I think you should start spending your money on something that will make you happy."

He frowned. "I am happy."

Valerie shook her head firmly. "No, you're not. And ever since you bought that painting it's even more obvious. You get this expression on your face whenever you look at it, like . . ." Her voice trailed off.

"Like what?" he asked in spite of himself.

"Like you want something you can't have. And that's not the look of a happy man."

Keith slid his hands into the pockets of his three thousand dollar suit. "I see. And your solution to this supposed problem is to throw money at it? That's not like you. You usually encourage me to throw my money at hospitals and homeless shelters."

"Yes, and I'm not going to stop doing that. But it wouldn't hurt for you to spend something on yourself." She gestured towards the painting, a portrait of a young woman. "I was actually glad when you bought this thing, because you wanted it so much and I thought it would make you happy. But it hasn't. So my advice is to spend a few weeks just . . . you know, indulging yourself. Go to Paris or London or some city you love. Spend obscene amounts of money for world-famous chefs to cook your favorite dishes. Pay high-class escorts to fulfill your wildest sexual fantasies."

He raised an eyebrow.

"Okay, so I was joking about the last part. But you could indulge in a few crazy one-night stands."

"What makes you think I'm not doing that already?"

Valerie rolled her eyes. "Oh, please. I've been your assistant for three years. I can tell when you're getting laid. The last time was . . ." She frowned, thinking. "Two months ago? No—two and a half. That advertising exec, what was her name? Horrible woman. I hated her guts."

This conversation was starting to bug him a little. "Her name was Emily, and she wasn't horrible."

"She was cold as ice and totally ambitious. The worst possible match for you. I just thank God she dropped you for that idiot senator. But whatever. I don't really care what you do, as long as you do something. You've been coming to the museum every day to stare at that painting, and you're starting to look a little . . ." She hesitated.

"A little what?" he asked irritably.

"Grim. Dark. Foreboding. And frankly, it's getting old. I feel like I'm working for Heathcliff and Mr. Rochester and Edward Cullen all rolled up into one."

"Edward Cullen?"

"Pop culture reference. He's a vampire. He broods."

"So if I stop brooding, you'll leave me alone?"

Valerie sighed. "I just wish you'd figure out the one thing in the world that would make you absolutely, ecstatically happy—and go after it."

His gaze returned to the painting. "I'll take it under advisement. Now, if you wouldn't mind actually earning your salary, I'd appreciate it if you'd go to the auction we were discussing and bid on that first edition."

"Fine, fine. What are you going to do?"

"Figure out what would make me absolutely, ecstatically happy. Which may turn out to be firing you."

She grinned at him. "You wouldn't last a week without me. Later, boss."

He listened to the efficient clicking of Valerie's heels as she walked across the marble floor, leaving him alone in the big gallery. He actually would have a hard time functioning without her. She was efficient and irreverent and smart as a whip, and the fact that she was a lesbian was a bonus.

As an extremely well-heeled bachelor, he often had to deal with female employees who had decided he was the husband of their dreams. It was a relief to know there was at least one woman in his life without romantic designs on him. All he had to deal with from her was an annoying tendency to fuss over him like an overprotective sister.

As he stared at the portrait in front of him, he wondered what Valerie would say if he told her that once upon a time, he'd actually known what would make him absolutely, ecstatically happy.

Sarah Harper.

The portrait had been painted by her father, the famous artist, and he had captured his subject perfectly. Sarah had looked exactly like this in high school. Beautiful and intelligent, with a face like eager flame behind a veneer of shyness.

He'd never been able to break through that shyness. All his life, his money and good looks had been enough to charm everyone he met . . . except for Sarah. She was the only girl who'd ever haunted his dreams, and he'd never made a dent in her reserve. During the four years they'd gone to high school together he could hardly get her to talk to him, much less go out with him.

They'd graduated and gone on to different colleges, and for the most part Keith had forgotten about her. But every so often she'd pop into his head, always with a hot surge of remembered lust. Something about Sarah had just . . . done it for him, and even years later the memory of her could still affect him. So when Julian Harper passed away and a few of his unsold paintings showed up in art auction catalogues, Keith paid attention. His own father had died six years ago, leaving him an enormous fortune, and now, for the first time, he was actually glad he had nearly unlimited funds at his disposal. They enabled him to buy the portrait he was looking at right now.

Sarah was sitting on an overstuffed sofa with her feet tucked up under her. She was wearing a green dress exactly the color of her eyes, and her long mahogany hair was loose around her shoulders.

He wished he could have brought the painting home right away, but the auction house's arrangement with the Harper estate included a month-long showing at the museum before the purchaser could take possession. He still had one week to go before the portrait would be his.

"The museum will close in fifteen minutes," the p.a. system announced.

Keith checked his watch. Considering how much money he'd donated to this place over the years, the staff probably wouldn't kick him out at closing time if he wanted to stay. But he'd been here for more than an hour already. It was time to go home.

He turned to do just that, and froze.

Sarah Harper was standing in the middle of the gallery, looking right at him.

***

Sarah's body flushed hot, as though she'd stepped under a heat lamp. Keith Logan was standing just a few yards away. She recognized him immediately, even though it had been ten years since she last saw him.

Her first instinct was to run and hide, as if she were a little girl instead of a grown woman. Her eyes actually went to the exits, as if she were planning her getaway.

Then she took a deep breath. What was she thinking? She needed to pull herself together and go say hello.

And she would. Any second now.

Move, feet. Move.

If she'd been prepared to see him, she would have taken the time to put on emotional layers of protection—enough to cultivate a polite, relaxed demeanor and a friendly smile. But as it was, she felt awkward and exposed, as if she were back in high school again with a secret crush on the most unattainable guy on the planet.

Her palms were actually sweating.

Okay, enough. She managed to put some kind of smile on her face as she forced her legs to carry her forward.

"Keith. Wow. It's been a while, huh?"

His face was completely blank, which was a little disconcerting. "Sarah. Hi."

When he held out his hand she would have killed for the chance to wipe hers on her jeans before she took it.

But Keith didn't seem to notice that her palm was sweaty. His fingers tightened around hers in a warm grip, and a shock of awareness went through her. She wondered if he could sense how fast her heart was suddenly beating.

She pulled her hand away with a jerk, and then blushed. She was acting like an idiot in front of the man who had paid a million dollars for one of her father's paintings.

She looked up at the painting in question. If it had been left to her, she would never, ever have sold it. But the portrait, along with everything else, had gone to her stepmother.

"So I heard you, um, bought this," she said, wincing inwardly at the inanity of the statement.

When Keith didn't say anything, she glanced at him again. He was looking at her, not the painting, with a kind of focused intensity in his blue eyes.

She wondered if she had a foam mustache from the cappuccino she'd drunk earlier. The urge to brush a thumb over her upper lip was almost unbearable, but she remembered what her therapist had told her about that kind of self-consciousness.

It wasn't a reflection of reality. Let it go.

Maybe Keith was just comparing the way she looked now to the way she looked in the portrait.

"He, um, painted that the summer before I went to college. So of course I look older now."

His gaze didn't waver. "I was thinking you look exactly the same."

She did? Was that good or bad?

Keith, on the other hand, didn't look exactly the same.

He looked better.

Broad shoulders in a perfectly tailored suit. Black hair, blue eyes, chiseled features. And most of all, a sense of controlled masculine power that sent a tickling sensation to the corners of her body—the insides of her elbows and the soles of her feet and the hollows behind her knees.

Just like in high school, her intense awareness of Keith Logan made her blush like a furnace. She may have made huge strides in dealing with her social anxiety disorder in the last several years, but right now, at this moment, it felt like she was seventeen again.

Time to go, Sarah.

She opened her mouth to say a polite goodbye.

"Have dinner with me tonight."

She stared at him, her mouth still open. He'd spoken the words abruptly, without smiling, which made her wonder if he'd felt obligated to ask—because they'd known each other in high school, or because of the painting, or something.

"Oh . . . that's nice of you, Keith, but I . . ."

"Do you have plans?"

Still abrupt, and still no smile. His blue eyes narrowed a little as he studied her, and something about that focused gaze made her answer honestly. "No, I was just going home."

"To write?"

He knew she was a novelist? "Well . . . yes." She wrote historical fiction, and was currently working on a story set in ancient Ireland. "My editor is expecting the first draft next month, so I have to keep my nose to the grindstone."

"You need to eat, though. Right?"

This was starting to feel surreal. Keith Logan, one of the richest men in the city—not to mention the guy she'd had a crush on all through high school—was pushing her to have dinner with him.

"Um..."

"We'll go around the corner to Michael's." Then he held out his arm.

In a daze, she took it.

The feel of his strong, suit-covered bicep under her hand was so distracting that she stumbled on the edge of the carpet in the museum lobby. Immediately that powerful arm was even closer, around her waist.

"Okay?" he asked.

She looked up to tell him she was fine, but the words caught in her throat.

He was so close she saw the shadow of stubble on his jaw, and the scar on his left temple she remembered from high school. He was so close she caught the faint scent of really expensive cologne.

He was so close she felt the warmth of his body through his elegant suit.

"Yes," she finally managed to say. "I'm fine."

Except that she wasn't. She wasn't anywhere close to fine.

But it was just dinner. An hour, maybe an hour and a half.

She could get through one meal with this man, no matter how awkward and self-conscious she felt around him. It would be a kind of milestone. If she could deal with this, it meant she could deal with any social situation.

One dinner was nothing. One dinner, and then she'd never see Keith Logan again.

* * *

He couldn't let this be the last time he saw her.

And yet he knew by the time their entrees came that she wouldn't go out with him again. He'd asked, casually, what she was doing that weekend, and she'd said she was busy. No details—just that she was busy. When he'd asked more specifically if she wanted to get together for coffee sometime—because everyone had an hour for coffee, right?—she said no, thank you. Again, no explanation: just that polite no thank you.

Quick and clean. The perfect brush off.

He'd brushed off plenty of people in his life—including many, many women—but he'd never been on the receiving end. People didn't brush off billionaires. It just didn't happen.

He'd surprised her into having dinner with him, but she wasn't going to let him catch her off guard again. No, Sarah Harper had apparently decided that this was a one-off, never to be repeated.

It wasn't because she disliked him—or at least, he didn't think so. She seemed interested in their conversation when he stuck to neutral topics—books and music and art—and she even smiled a few times. She seemed a little tense and uncomfortable, but she'd always been like that, and not just around him. Sarah had always been shy.

Maybe that was it. Maybe she just felt shy. Maybe if he dropped the whole second date thing and just kept her talking, she'd loosen up enough to agree to go out with him.

Because he wanted to see her again. He wanted that with an intensity that pulsed through him like a heartbeat. He'd half hoped that going to dinner with her would be anticlimactic, that he would discover his attraction to Sarah had faded over time . . . but that's not what happened.

As he watched the gleam of candlelight in her brown hair and noticed how it set off the creamy translucence of her skin, his body reacted to her exactly the way it had in high school.

He wanted her.

Something happened to him when he was with her. Something primitive. His body hardened and tightened; his skin prickled with lust and adrenaline. On the surface he was still civilized, but it felt like he was hanging on to that veneer by a thread. Just below the surface, another part of him was howling like a wolf.

He wasn't sure why Sarah brought this out in him. It wasn't like she made any kind of effort to drive men crazy. She was wearing a pair of jeans and a gray cotton shirt—neat and clean and comfortable-looking, but not flashy or seductive in any way.

And yet he couldn't take his eyes off her.

There was a pause in their conversation as the waiter brought their dessert, and he took the opportunity to ask about something that had been puzzling him.

"If you don't mind my asking, why did you let that particular painting go to auction? You didn't feel a sentimental attachment to it?"

Her face flooded with color. "It wasn't up to me. All my father's unsold work went to my stepmother when he died."

Keith frowned. "He didn't leave you anything at all?"

Sarah avoided his eyes as she ran a fingertip around the rim of her water glass. "My father always believed that kids should have to struggle—especially if they want a career in the arts. Once I graduated from college, I was on my own. I understood that. I was fine with it. It was part of my father's philosophy."

"Bullshit."

That startled her enough that she actually met his eyes again. "What?"

"Sorry. But it is bullshit. Leaving you that portrait wouldn't have made a difference to you financially. You wouldn't have sold it, would you?"

"Of course not." Her voice trembled a little, and then, suddenly, words burst out of her in a torrent. "I love that painting. My father wasn't the kind of man who could express his feelings verbally, but he put his heart and soul into his work and . . . and when I look at that portrait, I feel connected to him. Of course I wouldn't have sold it. The truth is, I expected him to leave it to me. It never occurred to me that he wouldn't. I thought he knew how I felt about it. But . . . he was starting to forget things, these last few years. I was worried he was developing Alzheimer's but Lexie—my stepmother—said he was fine and refused to let me take him to a doctor. Maybe when he made his will he just . . . forgot."

Forgot his own daughter? You weren't supposed to speak ill of the dead, but if the guy could forget a girl like Sarah, he was an idiot.

"What about your stepmother? She could have given it to you, couldn't she?"

Sarah took a bite of her caramel custard before answering. "Lexie and I aren't exactly close. I did ask her about the painting once, but . . ." She shrugged. "Anyway, what's done is done. In the grand scheme of things, I suppose it doesn't matter. It's just an object, right?"

Keith didn't answer her. A crazy idea had come into his head. An insane, impossible, lunatic idea.

He took a deep breath and let it out slowly. He remembered all those things Valerie had said—that he should go after whatever would make him happy. That he should pay obscene amounts of money just to indulge himself.

It had never occurred to him to actually follow her advice. But why shouldn't he, just once, use his wealth to get the one thing in the world he really wanted? Would it be so bad to indulge this one forbidden fantasy—the fantasy that for all the years of his adolescence had found its way into every single jerk-off session?

The fantasy that Sarah Harper was in his bed. At his mercy. That he could spend hours . . . even days . . . doing things to her until he broke through her defenses and she gave into him completely.

It was crazy. And it would never happen. But if he had even one shot in a million, he was going to take it.

It wasn't like he had anything to lose. She'd already made it clear she didn't want to see him again. So what if she shot him down and left in disgust? The end result would be the same. If he was never going to see her again, did it really matter if she spent the rest of her life thinking of him as some guy she'd gone to high school with, or some guy who was so desperate for her he'd tried to bribe her into his bed?

He'd only had one glass of wine with dinner, but suddenly he felt drunk.

Shit. Was he really going to do this?

Sarah finished the last bite of her custard, and used her tongue to catch a drop of caramel sauce at the corner of her mouth. A strand of hair fell over her cheek and she lifted a hand to brush it back.

And then all he could think about was Sarah in his bed with that long brown hair spread out on his pillow.

What would it take to make her gasp? To make her moan?

To make her beg . . .

Fuck, yes, he was going to do this.

* * *

What had possessed her to say all that to Keith? He didn't care about her screwed up family relationships. He was always so cool and contained and perfect, and she wasn't.

He'd been that way in high school, too. She'd blushed and stammered her way through four years of hell while he'd sailed along effortlessly, smart enough to get good grades, rich and handsome enough to get any girl he wanted, and polite enough to treat even outcasts like her with kindness. He'd always gone out of his way to be nice to her, even when his friends rolled their eyes and made snide comments.

She had a sudden memory of their English class senior year. She'd sat in the desk behind his, and she'd spent the semester staring at the back of his head, at his black hair and broad shoulders and powerful back, and the way his arm muscles bunched and released as he read or wrote or raised his hand. He'd dated a few different girls that year, and Sarah had hated every one of them with a wholly unjustified ferocity. She had no reason to hate those girls except that they had Keith Logan's strong hands all over their bodies.

What would it be like to see behind that cool perfection? To be the one who could make those icy blue eyes turn hot with lust?

It was so hard to picture that Sarah wondered if, even in bed, Keith Logan stayed cool. That was easier to imagine. She could visualize him making a girl lose control while he stayed in charge.

She sighed as she finished her dessert. Dinner hadn't been too bad, all things considered, but it would be a relief to say goodnight. Being with Keith made her too anxious, and she hated reliving the feeling that had defined her adolescence: longing for something she could never have.

"Sarah."

She glanced up at him, admiring the way the candlelight drew out a gleam in his blue eyes. In this light they looked almost navy.

"Yes?"

"What if I told you there was a way you could have that painting?"

For a moment she just stared at him. What could he possibly . . .

Oh, no.

"If you're thinking about giving it to me, just forget it. There's no way, and I mean none, that I would let you do that. I didn't tell you all that stuff about my family to make you feel sorry for me, if that's what you're thinking."

She sounded almost fierce when she made that little speech, and Keith raised his eyebrows.

"I wasn't thinking that. And I'm not planning on giving you the portrait. Far from it."

She frowned. "I can't afford to pay you a million, and selling it to me for what I *could* afford—maybe ten thousand, if I'm lucky—would be the same as giving it to me for free. I'm not your charity case, Keith."

He was smiling at her now. "I hardly ever got to see this side of you in high school," he said.

She refused to be charmed by the famous Keith Logan smile. "What side?" she asked gruffly.

"This side. I remember you jumped all over Mark Sullivan once, because he said it didn't matter if public schools had arts and music programs."

He remembered that?

"He was implying that kids from working class families wouldn't appreciate 'the finer things in life'."

"Mark was an asshole."

"Yes, he was. But I don't think *you're* an asshole. I just don't want you to think I—"

"I am an asshole."

She stared at him. "What?"

"I am. Whatever good opinion you might have about me, I'm about to destroy it."

"What are you talking about? How?"

"With the offer I'm about to make you."

"What offer?"

He leaned across the table. "The museum has the portrait for one more week. When the week is up, I'll have the painting delivered to you. I'll transfer ownership to you legally. It will be yours."

"I told you, Keith, I—"

"Don't you want to hear my price before you reject it?"

She sat back in her chair and folded her arms. "Fine."

"In exchange, for one week, you'll live with me in my house. During the day, you can do whatever you want. There's a gym, an indoor pool, a library, a home theater. There's a study where you can write, and my chef will cook you anything you want to eat. But at night..."

He paused for a moment. "At night, you have to do whatever *I* want."

For a minute, it just didn't compute. She sat frozen in place, staring at him, while her mind flailed around helplessly trying to process what she'd just heard.

Keith's face wasn't helping. He looked like he always did—cool, calm, collected. His eyes were maybe a little more intense than usual, and as she stared at him, she caught the twitch of a muscle at the corner of his jaw.

After what seemed like a long, long time, she was able to force out a question.

"Are you serious?"

"Yes."

It still didn't compute. Was it possible that what he'd meant and what she was thinking weren't the same? As humiliating as it would be to ask, she had to know for sure.

Her heart was thudding against her chest. "When you say *whatever you want*—do you mean—are you referring to—do you mean sexually?"

Oh, God. Had she really just asked that? Was this conversation really happening, or was she lying in a hospital bed hooked up to a morphine drip, recovering from a car accident or a fall down the stairs?

One corner of his mouth lifted slightly. "Yes."

She couldn't sustain her current heartbeat and live. Her pulse was roaring in her ears, and she seemed to be staring at Keith through a kind of mist. Her whole body was buzzing and vibrating, like an engine being pushed too far.

She grabbed for her water glass and spilled some on the table. "Shit."

That corner of his mouth rose a little higher. "I think that's the first time I've ever heard you swear."

She took a quick gulp of water and set the glass back down. It still seemed impossible that he was serious about this, but . . . what if he was?

What if he was?

And then she had a realization as astonishing as the offer.

She wanted to accept. And not because of the painting. She wanted to accept because she'd wanted Keith Logan from the moment she'd laid eyes on him, back in freshman year at Adamson Academy.

But a man who was offering a million dollar painting in exchange for her sexual favors would surely expect more than she could ever provide. He would expect moves. He would expect tricks. He would expect *something*.

And then suddenly she was talking. She was talking in a rush about things she never, ever talked about. She was staring down at the white table cloth and the spot where she'd spilled the water, telling Keith Logan about her sexual history.

Such as it was.

"Look. Before you get any ideas about me, you need to know something. I've had two boyfriends in my entire life, and I only slept with one of them. And it sucked. Okay? It totally sucked. It hurt and I didn't know what I was doing and it *sucked*. For both of us. So we broke up, and I decided that the whole sex thing just isn't for me. I have, so to speak, a solo gig as far as all that's concerned. It's just me and my trusty vibrator. Do you understand what I'm saying here? I don't have the first clue what I'm doing in bed. I'm not exciting, I'm not adventurous, and I have no skills. I'm not the kind of woman you want for this . . . arrangement of yours."

She paused to take a breath, her stomach clenching in agonized embarrassment at the truths that had just spilled out of her.

"I don't want skills."

Her gaze jerked up to meet his. "Then what *do* you want?"

A wicked gleam came into his eyes. "I want you in my bed and at my mercy. And I want to ruin you for your vibrator."

His voice was low and raspy and the sexiest thing she'd ever heard.

This couldn't be happening. It couldn't.

There had to be something wrong with this scenario. What if he was into really freaky stuff? Stuff she could never, ever deal with?

She cleared her throat and stared down at her empty dessert plate. "What if you did something I didn't like? I mean . . . would I have to stay no matter what?"

He didn't answer her right away, and after a minute she looked up again. He was staring at her with a blank expression on his face. "Sarah. Are you actually considering saying yes?"

What did *that* mean? Was this whole thing a joke after all?

"Oh, God. You weren't serious, were you? Of course not. What an idiot I am. What a total—"

"*Sarah.*" One of her hands was fisted on the table, and now he reached out and covered it with his.

Sensation shot up her arm and through her whole body. His hand was warm and big and strong, and little pulses of pleasure emanated from where they touched.

"I've never been more serious about anything in my life. So let me answer your question." He leaned towards her again. "If something happens that you don't like, all you have to do is say so. You can call off the deal anytime. To get the painting, you have to stay with me the whole week, and you can't say no to anything. If you do say no, or if you want to leave, the only consequence is that you don't get the painting. That's it."

His hand was still on hers, and she found herself lost in his blue eyes. How many times in high school—and long afterwards—had she fantasized about being in Keith Logan's bed?

Her skin prickled with heat and desire.

He thought the only reason she would ever agree to this was because of the painting. But the painting had nothing at all to do with what she said next.

"Okay."

For a second he just stared at her. Then his hand tightened on hers.

"You mean that?"

"Yes. I'll do it."

Saying the words filled her with a kind of recklessness she'd never experienced before. She felt wild, like she might be capable of anything.

When the wave of recklessness was followed by a wave of anxiety, she reminded herself that she could call off the deal anytime.

The waiter came to their table with the check, and Keith let go of her hand. He took care of the bill, and then he met her eyes again. "I'll send a car for you tomorrow afternoon. What's your address?"

As she gave it to him in a shaky voice, she wondered what in the hell had gotten into her—and how long it would take to wear off.

CHAPTER 2

Keith had no idea how he got through the next day. He was useless for all practical purposes, and when Valerie finally asked what was wrong he just shook his head.

"Would you believe I'm actually taking your advice?"

"Yeah? It's about time. What advice, specifically?"

"It's a long story. I'll see you tomorrow at the board meeting."

He'd forced himself not to call his housekeeper about Sarah until now, when he was finally heading home for the night. He'd told himself that by not asking, he was at least giving himself one day to hope and anticipate, even if she decided not to go through with it after all.

But now, as he slid behind the wheel of his Jaguar, he pulled out his cell phone and dialed home.

"Yes, Mr. Logan?"

"Hi, Nancy. I was just calling to find out if Miss Harper arrived this afternoon."

"Oh, yes, she's settled in nicely."

He was filled with a relief so intense he felt almost light-headed. "Good. Great. How did she spend her day?"

"Well, she put her things in the guest room you'd told me to prepare for her, and I brought her a plate of cheese and crackers and a glass of Burgundy. She wandered around the house a little and spent a lot of time looking at your art collection in the upstairs gallery. Then she went into the downstairs study with her laptop and did some work. She had dinner about an hour ago."

"Did you give her my letter?"

"Yes. With the dessert, just like you asked. She went to her room after dinner, and I heard her filling the bathtub a few minutes ago."

His mind filled with the image of Sarah taking a bath in his house, and he almost drove off the road.

"Okay. That's good. I don't think we'll need anything else tonight, Nancy. Why don't you head home?"

"All right, Mr. Logan. Do you want Paul to stay?" Paul was her husband, and also his chef.

"No. I had a late lunch and I'm not really hungry."

"We'll see you tomorrow morning, then."

So when he pulled into his garage and went inside the sprawling mansion, he knew that he and Sarah were alone in the house.

It was eight-fifteen. He'd told her in his letter that he would come to her at nine o'clock, so he couldn't cheat and go now, even though his heart was pounding and she was all he could think about. But he was the one making the rules, and he wasn't going to break them.

So he went to his bedroom suite instead, loosening his tie as he climbed the stairs and pulling his clothes off as soon as he was in the room. Then he turned on his Jacuzzi shower and let the hot water beat down on his naked skin. He resisted the urge to jerk off for the hundredth time that day, even though he was starting to think he probably should, just to take the edge off.

Because he was so hard right now his cock could crush diamonds. He hoped Sarah had followed orders and put on the blindfold he'd left for her, because he was afraid the sight of his lust-crazed expression and raging hard-on might make her rethink their agreement, given how inexperienced she was.

And he was afraid that despite his promise, if she told him she wanted to leave, he wouldn't be able to let her go.

* * *

Sarah tried not to think about nine o'clock. Every time she did, a wave of anxiety made her stomach tighten and she wanted to run back home.

She didn't know what gave her the courage to stay. Maybe it was Keith's letter, which had been oddly reassuring.

At nine o'clock precisely, be on your bed in the blindfold you'll find under your pillow. You can wear whatever you want. And remember that you can't do anything wrong, because I'm in charge.

Had he guessed about her ever-present fear of doing something wrong? Or was her neurosis just really obvious?

Sarah took her time in the bath, shaving her legs carefully and trying not to think about Keith touching them later. Even with his reassurance, if she thought too much about what might happen tonight she knew she'd chicken out.

By the time it was ten minutes to nine she was so nervous her hands shook as she got dressed. She agonized over the decision of what to wear, and finally chose her favorite pajamas over the more risqué set she'd bought that morning at a boutique downtown.

She'd always secretly thought that she looked sexy in these, even if she'd had them for years. Something about the cut of the white cotton camisole top made her small breasts look firm and shapely and perfect. The bottoms were thin and soft from many washings, and felt wonderful against her silky smooth, just-shaved legs.

Underneath she wore the white satin panties she'd bought that morning. They were simple and elegant and made her butt look amazing, which she supposed was some justification for spending thirty dollars on underwear.

Five minutes to go. Something told her Keith would be punctual. She sat down on the four-poster bed, brushing her fingertips over the burgundy silk comforter. The blindfold she'd found under the pillow was silk, too—a simple black band she'd tried on earlier.

Three minutes to go. She looked around at the beautiful room—the antique furniture, the Aubusson carpet, the fireplace and the artwork on the walls and the floor to ceiling windows hung with burgundy velvet drapes.

One minute to go. She lay down in the center of the bed, resting her head on the pillow and sliding the blindfold over her eyes. Her heart was beating so hard she could hear it.

And then she heard the door open.

Her hands fisted involuntarily, and she found herself clutching the comforter. For a minute there was silence, and then she heard footsteps coming towards her.

A wave of goose bumps prickled her skin. She felt the bed give as a large male body sat down on the edge, and every muscle in her body tightened.

She heard a match striking, and there was a faint whiff of sulfur. Then she caught the sweeter scent of wax, and realized that Keith had lit the white candle on her bedside table.

"Candlelight becomes you."

His voice was low and raspy, like last night when he'd said he wanted her in his bed.

Was she supposed to say something in answer? A spasm of anxiety tightened her stomach muscles. She had no idea what the rules were, what he expected of her, what she was supposed to—

And then she remembered his letter.

You can't do anything wrong, because I'm in charge.

If he wanted her to speak, he could say so, or ask her a question. But since he hadn't done either of those things, she could do what she wanted.

And she wanted to stay silent. She wanted to take in everything that was happening, the sound of his voice and the scent of the candle and even her own nervousness. She had no idea what was going to happen next, but it was up to Keith and not her.

All she could do was wait.

"You mentioned last night that you like sweet wine, so I brought a bottle of that Hungarian Tokay I told you about."

He slid an arm behind her shoulders and helped her to sit up.

"Try this," he said softly, and then she felt the rim of a glass touch her mouth. She parted her lips, and Keith tilted the glass very slowly until she could take a sip.

It was like drinking light—so sweet and sinful she felt half-drunk from just a taste. She parted her lips again, hoping for more, and Keith gave a low chuckle as he tilted the glass again.

She took a bigger sip this time, relishing the way the wine bloomed on her tongue as it slid down her throat.

Then the glass was gone and something else took its place.

Keith's mouth was on hers.

It wasn't a kiss as much as a whisper of satin. The brush of his lips left hers tingling, and when he did it again she actually leaned into it.

The arm around her shoulders tightened, and his other hand slid into her hair. The pressure of his mouth was firmer now, and when she felt his tongue trace the seam of her lips she parted them eagerly.

And then he took her mouth for his own. His tongue was everywhere, stroking her until she felt it between her legs. Her heartbeat was thundering in her ears. The sensations were so overwhelming that she pulled back with a gasp.

Then she panicked. She'd pulled away. Was that allowed? No—it couldn't be. He'd said she had to do everything he wanted.

"Sarah."

His arm slipped from behind her shoulders and he settled his hand on her hip. She tensed up, waiting to hear what he would say next.

"There may be times this week when you say no or pull away but don't really want to end our deal. So when you say no or pull away, I'm going to ignore it. You might like the way that feels. But we'll need a way for you to tell me if you really *do* want to end our deal. So if you're serious about wanting me to stop whatever I'm doing, then I want you to say . . ." He hesitated a moment. "Abstract Expressionism. If you say that, then I'll stop, and we'll be done. Okay?"

He'd given her a way to freak out without ruining everything. She relaxed in relief, and nodded. "Okay."

"So let's try this out," he whispered, leaning close.

One of his big hands brushed up her arm, over her shoulder, into her hair. His thumb stroked the sensitive skin of her earlobe, and when she shivered in pleasure he did it again.

Then his other hand was on her left shoulder, and he slid one finger under her camisole strap.

A rush of sensation and anxiety made her stomach clench, and she felt herself stiffen.

"Tell me no," he said, and she realized that she wanted to. Not because she wanted him to stop, but because this was so new and intense she needed an outlet for her nerves.

"No," she whispered, and then Keith put his hands at the hem of her camisole and pulled it off so quickly she squeaked.

She covered herself instinctively, crossing her arms over her chest. Keith gripped her shoulders in his powerful hands and exerted steady, inexorable pressure to ease her down onto the bed. He grasped one of her wrists and pulled it up over her head, slipping something soft around it. He did the same thing to her other wrist. And then she was lying with her arms stretched over her head, her hands caught in velvet cuffs and her upper body naked.

Her heart thumped in her chest and her breath came in ragged pants. "Stop," she gasped, as Keith's mouth descended onto her breast. And then—"Stop," she said again, even as her back arched involuntarily to bring her closer to him.

His hand replaced his mouth, kneading firmly. "You can beg all you like, Sarah. I have no intention of stopping. Not until I've taken what I want."

Now both his hands were on her breasts, and it felt so good she squirmed, unable to stay still. She jerked against the handcuffs, and when she felt how securely they held her a flood of warmth surged through her.

His hands tightened until it almost hurt . . . almost but not quite. She wondered suddenly what it would feel like to cross that line, to move from pleasure to pain.

As soon as the thought crossed her mind she was ashamed of it. She didn't crave pain. She didn't want to be tied down like this. This wasn't her. This wasn't anything like—

And then the almost-painful grip was gone, and his tongue was there, drowning her in sensation as shockingly soft as his hands had been hard.

Oh, God. He sucked her nipple into his mouth, and she wished the rest of her could follow—that she could pour herself into him somehow. She did the closest thing she could and arched her back, and then Keith's hands slid under her shoulder blades and he held her suspended above the bed, swirling his tongue around her other nipple before biting down without warning.

It wasn't a hard bite but the shock went straight down her body, stabbing through her stomach and between her legs. Then he was soothing her with his tongue again, licking her softly and thoroughly. His hands slid out from under her, letting her settle down on the bed as he took her nipples between his fingers and thumbs.

He rolled the hard peaks back and forth with gentle pressure, and she felt it everywhere. He'd done something to her body—opened up a channel of sensation from her nipples to her—

Then he pinched her, hard, and the pleasure was so intense she cried out.

"Did you say something?" he asked softly.

"Stop, you have to stop," she said, even as the words turned into a moan.

Instead he pinched her again, not releasing her this time but holding her nipples tight even as he pressed a soft kiss against her throat.

He trailed his lips up her neck to her jaw line, and back down to her collarbones. On the way he touched his tongue to her skin in silken whispers.

And all the while he held her nipples in a hard, rough grip.

She was breathing in short little gasps, and she'd begun to twist underneath Keith's hands. She was feeling too much—too much pleasure and pain and everything in between, and in her core an aching blaze of want.

Keith withdrew his hands and his mouth, and Sarah's body quivered from the sudden loss.

And then he trailed one finger over the heart of her. "Your skin is so soft. Are you soft here, too?"

Oh, God. Would he be able to tell how wet he'd made her?

He touched her again, tracing the folds of her body through her pajamas, and she jerked away in a mingled rush of desire and mortification.

In the next instant he was holding her down, his hands like iron on her hips.

"You can't hide from me," he said in a low voice, and then he was tugging her pajamas and panties down her legs.

Goose bumps covered her bare legs and she actually fought against him, twisting onto her side and bending her knees against her chest. "Don't," she panted. "Please, don't."

"I'm going to see every inch of you."

He grabbed her lower legs, and then she felt the touch of velvet as he slipped the same cuffs around her ankles that he had used on her wrists.

Her legs were forced wide open, spread eagled in a V that exposed everything. Everything. All she could think was *my pussy, my pussy, my pussy* . . . a word she used in her internal monologues about sex, when she fantasized in her own bed at night—but had never used in conversation and tried not even to think when she was around other people.

But now it was all she could think about, because it was . . . *there*. On display. And as she lay still with no idea of where Keith was, since he wasn't touching her at the moment, she could only imagine that he was looking at her.

Looking at her pussy.

And as she imagined that, she became so painfully aware of how wet she was that hot color flooded her cheeks.

He still wasn't touching her. How did she look to him? What was he thinking?

The women he was usually with probably did the whole Brazilian wax thing. She went for regular bikini waxes, not because she expected a man to be spending any time down there but because swimming was her exercise and she spent three days a week in a bathing suit, even in the winter. So she was neat and trimmed but not . . . exotic.

He still wasn't touching her. Oh God, oh God, oh God. She was so much less sophisticated than the women he was used to. She'd been around women like that all her life, even if she'd been too crippled by her social anxiety disorder to be one of those women herself, and she'd always felt rough and unfinished next to their polished perfection.

She felt that way now. Rough and unfinished and exposed—literally.

And then, finally, Keith said something.

"Why, Sarah. I'm shocked."

His voice was low and husky, and the sound shivered along her nerve endings.

"You kept saying no, and all that time you were wet for me."

He trailed his finger over her again, but this time there was nothing between his skin and hers.

And then the most mortifying thing of all happened. His touch felt so good that she opened for him. The folds of her body parted with a little rush of honeyed moisture, and Keith's hand went still.

"Fuck," he whispered.

Every inch of her skin seemed to burn. She tried to squirm away from him, but he gripped her hip with one hand and covered her pussy with the other. "I don't think so," he said with a low chuckle. His big palm pressed against her, and when she squirmed again he pressed harder. And then, suddenly, she found herself digging her heels into the bed so she could bring her body closer to that insistent warmth.

"That's what I thought," he said, and she felt his body settling between her legs. "I'm going to taste you now, Sarah."

She froze. "Keith—no." It was the first time she'd used his name tonight. "I've never done that. I don't want to do that."

He used his hands to frame her, his index fingers on either side of her mound and his thumbs stroking softly over her tender skin.

"I'm going to do whatever I want to you. For as long as I want."

His thumbs pressed into her flesh as he parted her, and then his tongue stroked her inner folds in a slow, erotic slide.

Her body jerked as though she'd been shocked.

"Stay still," he ordered her.

"I . . . I can't."

One of his hands slid underneath her, and her whole body tensed when she felt the tip of his finger at her anus.

"Which would you rather have? My finger in your ass or my tongue on your pussy?"

Shit. "Your tongue!" she gasped.

"Where?"

She swallowed. "On . . . on my pussy."

His finger brushed lightly over her anus. "If you fight me, I'll fuck you here—with my finger if you're lucky and my cock if you're not. So I'd suggest staying very still while I eat you out."

Her heart thumped in heavy beats against her ribs. Keith put his hands on the sensitive skin of her inner thighs and caressed her softly from hip to knee, over and over, until the seductive gentleness of his touch became almost hypnotic.

No matter what happened, she would stay still. She could handle anything if it meant not having Keith's finger—or any other part of him—in her ass.

"Good girl," he said softly, and then his hands gripped her hips and his tongue was on her again.

Her cuffed hands fisted as she took a long, shuddering breath.

She'd fantasized about oral sex, of course. She'd fantasized about a lot of things she didn't do in real life. But her imagination hadn't prepared her for this.

His tongue was so soft. Like wet velvet. He was in no hurry at all, just licking her slowly and thoroughly until a low buzz of pleasure sparked deep in her bones.

She'd never experienced anything so . . . decadent. But how could this be enjoyable for him? Wasn't he tired of it yet? The longer it went on the more helpless and turned on she felt, and the more she wanted . . . *more*.

"Please," she heard herself say.

Immediately he stopped. "Please, what?"

She shifted restlessly, pissed at herself for saying something out loud and making him stop. "Please keep going."

"Exactly like I was? Or do you need something different? Something . . ."

He pressed his thumb against her clit, and it was so exactly what her body craved that she moaned.

"Something here?" he finished.

"Yes, oh yes..."

Her embarrassment had disappeared, along with her inhibitions, and she pushed her hips off the bed and into his touch.

"That's it," he said softly, and then he was on her again, fastening his mouth on her clit and tonguing her, sucking her, his sudden urgency like a match to tinder. The sensations built so fast that she cried out, her wrists and ankles straining against the handcuffs as her orgasm swept over her like a tidal wave.

Her whole body quivered as she came down from the most intense climax she'd ever experienced. Her heart thundered in her chest and she couldn't seem to catch her breath.

After a while she realized that Keith was kissing his way up her body, soft and slow. The sensation heightened the aftershocks rippling through her, and if she hadn't been chained up she might have floated right off the bed.

"Keith," she said, the word coming out like a sigh.

He kissed her on the mouth, quick and hard and possessive.

Her nerves were still tingling. What would happen now? She was in a frame of mind to submit to anything he asked of her.

The truth was, she was eager. Which was why his next words were such a bucket of cold water.

"I think that's enough for tonight," he said, and then he was undoing the cuffs at her wrists and ankles.

When her limbs were free he helped her to a sitting position. He slid an arm around her waist and kissed her again, softer this time. His upper body was bare but he was wearing bottoms—sweats or pajamas or something like that.

He hadn't even taken all his clothes off.

She felt disoriented and bewildered. "But . . . that can't be all. You didn't . . . I mean . . . nothing happened for you."

He chuckled. "I enjoyed myself thoroughly, Sarah. And I have you for a whole week. That means I can take my time."

He said that, but if he really wanted her he would have taken her. She'd been ready, willing, and chained up, for God's sake.

Her post-orgasmic bliss was fading, replaced by the much more familiar taste of anxiety.

"Keep the blindfold on until you hear the door close. Then you can take it off." He kissed her again, and she felt him get off the bed. "Have a good day tomorrow,

Sarah. You'll get another letter at dinner with your instructions. I'll see you at nine o'clock tomorrow night."

She heard his footsteps, and then the door closing.

After a minute she took the blindfold off and laid it down on the bed beside her. Then she stared at the closed door and tried not to feel bereft.

Why had he left like that?

The most obvious answer was also the most depressing. Because the simplest explanation was that he didn't want her. Not really. Not in that overpowering, I-must-have-you-or-I'll-die sort of way.

The way that she wanted him.

She threw herself back on the bed and stared up at the ceiling.

This was high school all over again. She wanted him, and he didn't want her. Only now that feeling was brutally heightened, because he'd brought her to such a state of ecstasy before walking away.

She sighed and rubbed her face with her hands. Now that she'd come down from that unbelievable high, she felt tired. She should get some sleep, and maybe things would look different in the morning.

She started to reach for her pajamas, and then stopped. She wanted to sleep naked tonight. Keith might have confused her by leaving when he did, but her body still retained the imprint of his touch and she wanted to savor that.

The lights were off but the candle was still burning. Now she leaned over and blew it out, settling back into the darkness and the softness of her bed, pulling the blankets up to her chin and cocooning herself into them.

The silk sheets felt wonderful against her bare skin.

CHAPTER 3

A gentle knock at the door woke her.
"Miss Harper?"

Sarah blinked and sat up, remembering when the blankets dropped to her waist that she was naked. She pulled everything up to her chin again.

"Yes?" she called out, uncertainly.

The door opened and the housekeeper she'd met yesterday stuck her head in the room. "It's just me," she said with a smile. "I wanted to find out if you need anything, and if you're ready for breakfast."

Sarah glanced around the room, but didn't see a clock. "What time is it?"

"Nine-thirty."

"It is? Wow. I never sleep that late. Um . . . breakfast. Yes. That sounds great."

"Would you like me to bring you a tray, or—"

"Oh, no, I'll come down," Sarah said quickly. She didn't want Nancy to think she was some kind of lady of leisure who had breakfast in bed every morning. "I'll, um, be down in half an hour."

"I'll let Paul know."

Paul was the chef, she remembered. "Okay. Great."

After Nancy closed the door again she got out of bed and headed for the bathroom.

* * *

It should have been a perfect day. Breakfast was delicious—crepes with lingonberries, sausage sautéed with mushrooms, and the best latte she'd ever tasted, with Paul pouring espresso and hot milk from two separate containers into her cup, so they flowed together in one perfectly foamy stream. After breakfast she brought her laptop down to the library she'd fallen in love with yesterday, settling down at the antique desk between two bays of leather-scented books and preparing to work hard for the next several hours.

Only she couldn't.

When she realized she'd been staring at her screen for ten minutes, she got up and started to pace.

The library was ideally suited to pacing. It was big and empty and quiet, and with the enormous oriental rug on the floor her footsteps didn't make any noise.

She never had trouble concentrating on her work. From the time she was a child, concentrating on books or writing had been her escape from the pressures of social situations. So why couldn't she focus now?

Because Keith had invited her into his home so he could have his way with her, and then he hadn't. He'd pleasured her to the point of levitation without taking his own pleasure.

And suddenly, out of nowhere, she was angry.

Was she so undesirable? Or was he deliberately trying to torture her? Was this just a game to him, some kind of—

Well, of course it was a game. He was a billionaire indulging a whim. Some kind of weird whim of arousing her sexually without getting aroused himself.

Suddenly she laughed. She imagined telling someone about her dire situation. "So this gorgeous billionaire I had a crush on in high school offered me a deal. He'll give me the one painting of my father's I've always wanted if I stay in his mansion for a week being totally pampered, with plenty of time and space to work on my book—as long as, at night, I let him go down on me and give me the most intense orgasms of my life without having to do anything for him in return."

She wondered how many women in the world would trade their problems for hers.

It sounded perfect. It sounded like something out of a fantasy.

But it wasn't *her* fantasy.

In her fantasy about Keith, the one she'd had since she was fourteen, there was some kind of connection between them. They told each other things they didn't tell other people. They understood each other in ways no one else did.

It was a lonely girl's fantasy. A fantasy as much about the need for human contact as it was about a teenager's crush.

Sarah stopped pacing. She found herself in front of a deep leather armchair, and she sank down into it with her feet tucked under her.

She had friends now—good friends. People she'd met in college, or through her writing. She still struggled with social anxiety but she'd fought through it to the point where she was capable of making real friendships.

She didn't need to visualize Keith in that role anymore. But that wasn't the only thing she'd imagined about him, in her bed at night with the lights off. She'd also lusted after him. She still did. So how did she see him, sexually speaking?

She leaned back into the butter soft leather as she replayed the events of last night.

Beneath the layers of nervousness and embarrassment, she'd been turned on.

Really, really turned on.

Be honest with yourself, her therapist liked to say. *Life's too short not to know your own heart.*

She closed her eyes and let her mind sift through her sexual fantasies, past and present. The truth was, she'd always imagined Keith taking charge like he had last night. So it seemed that her idea of him had some root in reality. Maybe she'd always known that side of him was there, and some equivalent part of her responded to it.

So why did she feel so unsatisfied now? He'd taken charge, hadn't he? He'd blindfolded her and chained her up, for God's sake.

While he hadn't even gotten naked.

That night at dinner, she'd imagined Keith staying cool while he made a woman lose control. And that's exactly what had happened.

Another rush of anger swept through her. Why should Keith get to stay safe while she was so vulnerable?

Well . . . maybe because he was the one who'd set this whole thing up. He was the one who made the rules. He assumed that what she wanted was the painting, and in exchange, what happened between them at night would be on his terms.

Suddenly restless, Sarah pushed herself up from the chair and started to pace again.

She didn't have to stay. She could go. She could pack up and leave right now. That was the control he'd given her—the ability to end their arrangement at any time.

The one thing she couldn't do was try to change the rules, or control anything that happened between them at night. So she couldn't demand that he have sex with her or anything like that.

The absurdity of that notion made her laugh out loud. Imagine the girl with social anxiety disorder saying to the billionaire, "I insist that you fuck me immediately."

No. That would never happen. Even if she could find the metaphorical balls to say such a thing—which was, in itself, impossible—it would violate the agreement between them. She could do whatever she wanted during the day, as long as she did whatever he wanted at night.

At night.

She glanced at the windows, hung with drapes to protect the rare books from direct sunlight. But the sunlight was out there. It was daytime.

Nighttime was off-limits—and, by extension, whatever happened between them sexually. But that didn't mean she couldn't call him right now. She wouldn't talk about their bargain or anything sexual. But she could reach out to him.

* * *

Maybe he should just take the week off. Tell his assistant he was unavailable for board meetings and conference calls and business lunches.

Because as long as Sarah Harper was under his roof, he was going to be useless. Completely fucking useless.

She was all he could think about.

Last night, after he'd left her, he'd gone to his suite and straight into the bathroom, where he'd stripped off his pajama bottoms and stepped into the shower to jerk off. Later in bed he'd jerked off again, but he still couldn't get to sleep. He wanted Sarah so much it felt like his blood was on fire. He wanted to go back to her room and fuck her senseless.

Why the hell hadn't he when he had the chance?

She'd been lying there waiting for him, chained and naked and flushed with the orgasm he'd given her. She was every wet dream he'd ever had. She was *the* wet dream, the one girl he'd never been able to have, tied down and at his mercy the way he'd imagined so many times. He could drive himself into her and purge all that frustrated lust, all that hopeless longing. Wanting something you couldn't have made you weak, and now he had the opportunity to take what he'd always wanted.

To take Sarah.

So why hadn't he?

Going down on her had been intense. Maybe too intense. He'd never been so turned on by turning a woman on, even though he loved to make a woman come and always had.

But this had been different.

Maybe that's why he'd left. Because this felt different, and he wanted to be sure he had a handle on what was going on before he got in any deeper.

He wanted to be sure he had a handle on himself.

He was in his office downtown, where he was supposed to be meeting the chairman of one of his boards in half an hour. He scrubbed his face with his hands as if he could get Sarah out of his head that way.

Because he had to get her out. He had to stop thinking about her. He had to compartmentalize this, to relegate her to the place she belonged, to—

His cell phone rang, and when he glanced at it he saw his home number on the screen. A sudden chill ran down his spine. Nancy was the only one who ever used that number. Was she calling to tell him that Sarah was gone?

"Yes? What is it?" he asked brusquely.

"Did you ever have a pet?"

It was Sarah's voice. So she was still there, at his house.

Relief made him sag back in his chair. "What?"

"I was wondering if you ever had a pet. During high school."

"A pet?"

"Yes. A dog, a cat, a bird, a fish. A pet."

It was so damn good to hear her voice. But what the hell was she talking about? "I . . . what?"

"I was wondering, because back in high school the headmaster had that dog, do you remember? I think it was a Jack Russell terrier. And whenever you saw it you'd go down on one knee and let him jump all over you and lick your face, even if you were dressed up. So I wondered if you ever had a pet of your own. Because you don't now. Or if you do, you keep it in some part of the house I haven't seen yet."

He blinked. "You're calling to ask if I ever had a pet?"

"Yes." Her voice sounded almost belligerent, as though she might be mad at him. Was this because of last night? Had she not enjoyed herself? It had seemed at the time like she really, really enjoyed herself, but maybe something else was going on.

"Are you upset with me for some reason?" he asked cautiously.

"No. Why? Do I need to be upset with you before I can ask a personal question?"

Definitely belligerent.

"Of course not. I'm just surprised to hear from you, that's all. And the question's a little . . ." He hesitated. The fact was, he didn't particularly want to talk about pets or the lack of them. Because it *was* a personal question. And talking to Sarah about personal things was not going to help him with his problem—this feeling that he was getting in too deep.

"Now's not a good time for me."

"Okay. When should I call back?"

He got up from his desk and walked over to the window. "Sarah."

"What?"

"I don't think we need to talk like this. Do you?"

"I don't know if we *need* to or not. I just know that I want to. If you don't, of course that's okay. But if that's the case then I'll be heading home today."

Panic swept through him, and he gripped the phone as if it was a part of Sarah's body. "If you leave now you won't get the painting."

"I know."

Panic was followed by anger. "Jesus, Sarah. Why does it matter if I had a pet growing up?"

"If you don't want to talk about that, I'll ask something else."

"Like what?"

"Who's your favorite artist?"

He closed his eyes briefly. Okay, fine. If this is what it would take to keep her with him, he could put up with it.

He took a deep breath. "Edward Hopper."

"Really?"

"Yes. Why do you sound so surprised?"

"I don't know. You have so many impressionists in your collection, and a lot of medieval art, too. I guess I expected your favorite artist to be more . . . traditional. Classic."

"Edward Hopper is classic."

"I guess you're right. A modern classic. So why do you like him so much?"

"I don't know. I just always have."

"What's your favorite painting by him?"

"*Nighthawks*," he said, glancing up at the reproduction framed on his wall.

"I love that painting. Why is it your favorite?"

He was starting to feel uncomfortable. Off-balance.

If they hadn't started a sexual relationship last night, he wouldn't feel this way. It wasn't like he hadn't had conversations like this before. It was a first date sort of conversation, and God knows he'd had plenty of those in his lifetime.

But this wasn't a first date. Sarah hadn't wanted to go on a first date with him, which was why he'd bribed her into their current arrangement. And because it would only last a week, after which he didn't expect to see her again, he'd figured he might as well indulge himself completely. Give into urges he didn't usually express.

Most of the women he dated weren't into what he was, or else they were a lot more hard-core. He hardly ever found the right balance with a bed partner.

He wasn't into the BDSM scene. He'd visited a club once, and realized immediately that there was nothing there for him. He liked to dominate in bed but he wasn't into pain—not that much pain, anyway—and what he saw at the club felt staged and artificial.

He didn't meet many women he clicked with sexually, so his dominant side didn't come out too often. And on the rare occasions he did click with a woman that way, there had never been any other connection. They'd been short, hot affairs that ended amicably enough, and that was it.

Without realizing it, over the years, he'd put sex and relationships into two different boxes in his mind. Now Sarah was muddying the waters.

Suddenly he felt angry. She'd established her boundaries with him that night at dinner, and that was fine. But then he'd established his boundaries for her, and she was ignoring them.

And threatening to leave.

"I have a meeting in a few minutes. Have we talked enough?" he asked brusquely, without answering her last question.

"Enough for what?"

"Enough to satisfy you. Enough that you'll still be there tonight."

There was a short silence, which gave him plenty of time to realize exactly how much he cared about the answer.

"Yes, I'll be here."

"Fine. You'll get your instructions at dinner."

He ended the call, and then immediately regretted his abruptness. There was nothing stopping Sarah from changing her mind.

And no guarantee she'd be there when he got home.

His assistant buzzed him to let him know that his two o'clock appointment had arrived. He took the meeting even though he felt tense and angry, hoping he'd be less knotted up by the end of it.

He wasn't.

Once he was alone in his office again he started to pace back and forth. The more he paced, the angrier he got.

After a while he sat down at his desk, pulled out his stationary, and started to write.

He'd left a letter with Nancy that morning, to be given to Sarah at dinner like the night before. But now he had new instructions for her.

If they scared her off, so be it. But if she stayed, there'd be no holding back tonight. He'd take exactly what he wanted from her.

He called for a messenger to deliver the letter to Nancy and then did everything in his power to forget about Sarah for the rest of the afternoon.

* * *

He stayed in his suit this time, and he made her wait. He had a dinner meeting with some people from St.

Luke's hospital, where he was funding a new wing, and he didn't leave the restaurant until eight forty-five.

It was nine-fifteen when he walked through the front door. Paul and Nancy had already gone home, so he and Sarah were alone—if she was still here.

He strode up the stairs without stopping at his suite, and stood outside her door for a minute. Then he set his jaw and pushed inside.

She was there. Relief flooded through him, followed by a wave of lust so intense it was almost painful.

She had followed his instructions, and was kneeling on the rug in front of the bed, naked and blindfolded. Her mahogany hair tumbled down her back, her lips were parted, and her hands rested on her bare thighs. As he closed the door behind him, he saw her hands fist briefly and then relax.

So she was nervous. Good. Then she knew what he'd been feeling for the last seven hours.

Adrenaline coursed through him as relief, desire, and anger coalesced into raw need. She looked so goddam sexy. Her nipples drove him crazy—small and pink and perfect. He remembered how they'd tasted last night, and the way his girl had shuddered when he bit and pinched them.

His girl? When had he started thinking of her as his girl?

She was here for exactly one week. She was most definitely not his girl.

He strode across the room until he stood right in front of her.

"Undo my belt and my zipper," he said, keeping his voice cool. He knew he was angry, and that a part of him wanted to punish her, but he didn't care.

If she decided to leave after tonight—or even during the night—there was nothing he could do to stop her. But if she decided to stay, she would damn well know who was the boss in the bedroom.

She reached up hesitantly and her hands met his thighs. He sucked in a breath as she groped her way towards his belt.

She found it. She explored the Italian leather for a moment and then undid the buckle slowly, her slender hands working precisely and carefully until she could slide it out completely and drop it on the floor.

Fuck. Something about the graceful efficiency of those small fingers made him hard as a rock. He felt off-balance, almost dizzy with desire. He opened his mouth to give another order, any order, with no purpose other than to assert his dominance—but then her fingers brushed over his erection as they settled on his fly.

All he could do was watch and try to stay upright as Sarah undid the button and lowered his zipper. She paused, and he knew that was his cue to tell her what to do next. But his mouth was dry and he couldn't utter a word. She hesitated, her face uncertain, but he still couldn't speak. A little frown gathered between her brows. Then her face cleared, and she gripped his pants and boxers in both hands and drew them down over his hips.

His erection sprang free and almost hit her in the face.

His hand shot out reflexively, and thank God one of the bedposts was within reach. He gripped it hard and somehow managed to keep from collapsing as Sarah touched him for the first time.

This was another point when he'd normally tell her exactly what to do, in a hard voice that made it clear who was in charge. But he didn't do that with Sarah. He was unbearably turned on by her tentative exploring and he couldn't bring himself to interrupt her.

It was obvious that while she'd probably done this a few times before, she wasn't experienced. There was a kind of shy curiosity on her face and in the way she touched him that he'd never encountered before.

Was it her inexperience that was so mesmerizing? Even as a teenager, he'd been with girls who knew what they were doing. He'd always thought that's what he preferred. So why was it so arousing to watch Sarah trail her fingers over his hard length, hesitantly at first and then with more confidence? Why did he have to grit his teeth to keep from groaning when she finally gripped him more firmly?

Then she touched her tongue to his head, tasting him, and it was a miracle he didn't snap the bedpost in two.

She was so cautious at first that he was caught between frustrated lust and a kind of fierce affection that was new to him. She was adorable. She was beautiful. And she was driving him insane.

She ran her tongue along his shaft, over and over, and then swirled it around his head before taking him into her hot, sweet mouth.

The sight of her lips wrapped around his cock short-circuited his brain. He'd fantasized about seeing her like this so many times, but he felt none of the triumph he'd always thought he would if he ever got Sarah naked and on her knees, with his dick in her mouth.

Instead he felt like he was standing at the edge of an abyss.

He needed to take control. He should tell her what to do, put his hand on the back of her neck to force her movements. *Harder. Faster. Deeper.*

But he couldn't. Her touch was so gentle, so hesitant . . . and yet it filled him with a pleasure so intense he vibrated with it. It was a strange, fragile ecstasy, and it scared the shit out of him.

And he couldn't do a thing but let it wash over him.

She was stroking the base of his cock with her hand while she took as much of him in her mouth as she could. Her long brown hair flowed down her back and over her right shoulder in a waterfall of silk, brushing over her right breast as she leaned forward. Her nipples were hard little peaks, and her whole body seemed flushed.

She was turned on. Christ, she was turned on.

He gripped the bedpost harder and tried to control himself. It was too much, too intense. He needed to end this. He should ram his cock into her mouth, forcing her to deep throat him.

But he couldn't do it. He couldn't do anything that might hurt or scare her.

Fuck.

Her movements were bolder now, and as she licked and sucked she suddenly made a little sound . . . an *mmmmm* of enjoyment that shot through him in a lance of pure heat.

His body tightened. He was going to come.

A strange panic seized him. He couldn't shoot in her mouth . . . not this first time. She wasn't ready for that.

He pulled away, but her hand still grasped him.

"I'm going to come," he said hoarsely. She leaned forward and put her mouth on him again, and it felt so good he closed his eyes.

When he tried to pull away again, she gripped the back of his thighs.

Shit. He'd let go of the bedpost, and when Sarah grabbed him he was thrown off balance. He went down on his backside as he caught his weight on his forearms.

Before he could recover his equilibrium she was between his legs, her hands on his hips as she licked and sucked him, her hair falling forward and brushing over his bare skin.

There was no stopping it. His body tensed with wild excitement before his orgasm slammed into him, and then he was shooting into Sarah's mouth as an explosion of ecstasy roared in his ears and melted his bones.

He groaned her name almost helplessly, again and again, as waves of pleasure pulsed through him. After what seemed like a long time he took a deep breath and let it out slowly, and became aware that Sarah was stroking her hands up under his shirt, which was still buttoned, and exploring the contours of his stomach and chest.

He was lying on his back with his weight braced on his elbows, and as he stared down at Sarah a spasm of terror squeezed his heart. She was naked and blindfolded and between his legs, having sucked him to near madness and brought him to one of the most intense orgasms of his life.

He felt undone.

She'd pushed his shirt halfway up his body in her exploring, but now she stopped and sat back on her heels.

"I want to take off the blindfold," she said almost shyly. "I want to see you." Then she reached up as though to suit action to words.

He jerked upright and seized her wrists in a grip so tight she cried out.

"No," he said, realizing how out of control this had unexpectedly gotten and how essential it was to reestablish boundaries.

"But Keith, I—"

"Don't say my name," he snapped. "You can address me as Sir."

He hardly ever demanded that his partners call him Sir. But when Sarah used his name another clutch of panic had made his heart tighten in his chest.

He couldn't stay, he realized suddenly. He needed to get the hell out of here and regroup.

And if she was still here tomorrow, things would have to be very different between them. He'd gone easy on her tonight for some inexplicable reason, but no more.

He pulled away and got to his feet, leaving Sarah on her knees in almost the exact position she'd been when he'd first come in.

"You were doing well until the end," he said coolly, straightening his clothes with shaking hands. "Unfortunately, trying to remove your blindfold was a direct violation of my orders. We'll have to deal with that tomorrow night. You'll receive your instructions at dinner."

He paused, looking down at her. Her beautiful face was turned up towards his. With her eyes covered it was difficult to read her expression.

He was filled with an urge to rip off her blindfold himself and take her into his arms, raining kisses on that soft, sweet mouth.

His hands tightened into fists.

"You can take off the blindfold once I'm gone."

And then he left, without bothering to say goodnight.

CHAPTER 4

As she finished another delicious breakfast, Sarah reflected on the fact that now, at least, she had the answer to one burning question.

She *could* turn Keith Logan on. Last night, she'd literally knocked him on his ass, and it was the sexiest thing that had ever happened to her. Whatever this was to Keith, it wasn't just a game where he pleasured her without taking pleasure himself, staying in absolute control of the situation. He'd lost control a couple of times last night, and she'd never relished anything more in her life.

She wanted to make him lose control again. But he'd made it clear at the end that he didn't want that.

She could understand. She could sympathize. She felt the same way herself . . . or at least, she had until two days ago.

But she was starting to enjoy the experience of not being in control. Well . . . maybe enjoy wasn't the right word. It wasn't like a nice cup of tea, or a rainy day indoors with an Agatha Christie novel.

It was raw. It was intense.

It was dangerous.

Dangerous to the way she'd tried to live her life since she was five years old. Dangerous to her self-imposed isolation. Dangerous to every idea she had about herself.

Keith had pushed her out of her comfort zone, and she felt more exhilarated, more alive, than she ever had before.

And she wanted to give him the same thing. This week they had together was an opportunity. A chance for both of them to step outside the cages they'd made for themselves—cages of loneliness.

Because Keith *was* lonely. She'd never been more certain of anything.

Maybe he'd even been lonely in high school. It seemed inconceivable—he'd always been surrounded by people fawning over him, including every pretty girl at the Academy.

And yet, the only time she'd ever seen him look truly happy had been those moments when he was playing with the headmaster's dog.

She wished she'd had the courage to talk to him back then. He'd given her plenty of openings. He'd always been friendly towards her, but she'd usually responded to his overtures with shrugs or monosyllables, so paralyzed with embarrassment she couldn't even meet his eyes.

Of course a big part of that had been her social anxiety disorder, which hadn't been diagnosed until her freshman year in college. And that wasn't her fault.

Sarah rose from the breakfast table and went to the library, where she wandered slowly around the room, looking at the leather-bound books without really seeing them.

She wouldn't blame herself for the past, but she wasn't a teenage girl anymore. She was a grown woman who saw things differently now, and who could make different decisions.

Another minute brought her to the leather chair in front of the fireplace. She threw herself into it and picked up the phone on the table beside it.

"Hello, Sarah."

Keith sounded almost resigned, as though he'd been expecting—dreading?—her call. Sarah smiled and settled deeper into the chair.

"Did you know I had a crush on you in high school?"

There was a brief, electric silence. "Are you kidding?" he asked after a moment.

"Nope. I'm surprised you don't have a hole in the back of your head, after all the time I spent staring at you in class."

"But you never talked to me in high school. You barely even looked at me."

"I had social anxiety disorder. I still do."

Another silence. How would he react to hearing that? She remembered a friend who'd struggled with bulimia telling her she never revealed that part of her history to men. "Men hate it when women have things wrong with them," she'd said. "Especially weird, psychological things."

Sarah had told her that plenty of men were capable of unconditional love. Of course she'd been speaking from hope, not from experience. For all she knew, her friend might be right.

But she knew in her heart that if she and Keith were going to get to the place she wanted them to be—even if it was only for this one week—then concealment wasn't an option. She had to be willing to show herself to him, and if that meant he rejected her, then so be it.

The silence went on for at least a minute. Then—"I had no idea."

"Neither did I, until a professor of mine in college figured it out and helped me find a good therapist. I've made a lot of progress in the last few years. But that's why it was hard for me to connect with people in high school. Why it's still hard. The truth is, it will probably always be hard. But I'm dealing with it."

"I always knew you were shy, but I didn't realize how much you were struggling. I wish I'd known." There was a pause. "Can I tell you a secret?"

Sarah blinked. "Um . . . sure. Of course."

"I used to make you blush on purpose. I knew if I said hi you would, so even when I knew you probably wouldn't say hi back, sometimes I did it anyway."

She didn't know what to make of that. "You made me blush on purpose?"

"Yeah."

"But . . . why?"

"Because it made you look so beautiful. That pink in your cheeks. It made me wonder what you'd look like blushing all over."

Her breath caught in her throat. Now it was her turn to be silent. She could feel a blush coming on right now, creeping up her chest and her throat and burning in her cheeks.

When Keith spoke again, his voice was low and husky. "In case you haven't figured it out yet, I had a crush on you in high school, too."

No. That wasn't possible. Was it?

"But . . . all those girls. They threw themselves at you. You could have anyone you wanted."

"Anyone but you."

Right, okay. That made a little more sense. "So you wanted me because you couldn't have me? Because I was a challenge?"

"Jesus. No." He paused. "Well . . . maybe a little, at first. But I'm not a fucking idiot. Do you think I couldn't figure out that you were special? That you were the smartest, most interesting girl in school? Even if you wouldn't talk to me, you did have to talk in class every once in a while. And I listened to you. You were passionate and brilliant and you actually gave a shit about things that mattered. How many high school kids can you say that about? I might not have been a prize back then but I give myself this much credit: I've always been able to recognize quality."

He sounded like he meant what he was saying.

He'd liked her in high school?

"I had no idea," she said, unconsciously echoing what he'd said a few minutes before.

She didn't know what to think about this. She couldn't really process it. Once again, everything she'd believed for years was called into question.

And then she heard herself blurt, "I used to watch you all the time. I went to your soccer and basketball games, when I could. You were good, of course. You were good at everything you did. But the only time I ever saw you look happy was when you were with the headmaster's dog."

When he spoke he sounded irritated. "You're obsessed with that damn dog."

That made her smile. "You never did tell me if you ever had a pet."

That brought on the longest silence yet. She had to force herself to stay quiet and let Keith break it when he was ready.

At last he did. "Fine. You want me to say I have a soft spot in my heart for animals? I do. You want me to say I was starved of any real affection growing up, and the only outlet I had was the headmaster's dog? Well, that's true, too. I had a rotten childhood. My mother died when I was a baby and my father was a cold, unfeeling bastard. Is that what you wanted to hear?"

His voice was angry. Really angry. But she'd asked for it, and so she didn't say a word.

"But don't get the idea that I need love now," he went on. "Or that I need to be saved or healed or whatever. I have more money and freedom than most of the human beings on this planet. I have everything I ever wanted." A short silence, and then his voice turned low. "I even got to fuck that pretty mouth of yours last night. So don't worry about me. I'm doing just fine." Another pause. "I'm done talking now, Sarah. If this wasn't enough to satisfy you then I guess you'll pack up and leave. There's nothing I can do about that. But if you stay, you should know that I'm not in the mood to be gentle tonight. But maybe you won't stay to find out just how rough I can be."

He disconnected the call, and for a long time Sarah sat still, without moving. Her skin was tingling.

There was no question she was going to stay.

In spite of what Keith had said, she did think he needed love. But that wasn't the only reason she was staying. The biggest reason was selfish.

She wanted him. There was no part of her that wasn't turned on by Keith Logan, and she wanted everything from him that he was willing to give her—even if it was only for one week.

And even if she was a little bit nervous about tonight.

* * *

Lie face down, naked and blindfolded, and wait for me.

That was it.

Sarah finished reading the letter and tucked it in her back pocket as Nancy brought out dessert. It was caramel custard.

"Mr. Logan said you like this," she said cheerfully.

It was the dessert she'd ordered that night at the restaurant. For a man who wanted to portray himself as cold and aloof, he could be remarkably thoughtful.

"Is he a good boss?" she asked suddenly, as Nancy set the dish down.

Nancy looked a little surprised at the question, but she answered readily enough. "Yes, he is. A wonderful boss."

She probably wouldn't get an answer to her next question, but she asked it anyway.

"Does he . . . have a lot of women over?"

Nancy smiled a little as she poured more espresso into Sarah's cup. "I shouldn't talk about that."

"Of course not. I'm sorry. I—"

"I shouldn't, but I will."

Sarah blinked.

"I've been with him five years, and yes, he's been with his share of women. And yes, sometimes they stay the night. But he's never had a woman living here."

She shouldn't be so happy to hear that—but she was.

"I'm not exactly living here. I mean . . . I'm only here for a week."

"Mmm."

She wasn't sure how to interpret that, but she figured she'd put Nancy on the spot enough for one night.

Lie face down, naked and blindfolded, and wait for me.

She'd followed instructions and was now lying on her bed as tense as a bowstring. She tried not to wonder what was coming. Everything they'd done so far she'd loved, but of course that was no guarantee she'd feel that way tonight.

She had to remember that no matter how drawn she was to Keith, how much she wanted to stay, if something happened she didn't like she could end it and walk away.

The door opened.

Her heart thumped as she listened to Keith crossing the room towards her. Then she felt the bed give as he sat on the edge beside her.

"Lay on my lap," he said, his voice cool and even.

Shit. Shit. Did this mean he was going to spank her, or something? Of course that was one of the possibilities that had occurred to her when she read his note, but she'd let herself hope that it wouldn't happen.

Maybe it wouldn't hurt very much. Maybe—

"Now." His voice was like a whip, and she knew she had to decide.

She rose up on her knees and moved towards him on the bed. She used her hands to feel where he was and then awkwardly laid herself down across his powerful thighs.

He was bare-chested but he was wearing pants—jeans, she thought. The denim was rough against her skin, and she felt an unexpected jolt of excitement.

Keith ran his big palm along her spine and down across her backside. He traced the curves of her buttocks with slow, gentle strokes, and suddenly she realized something.

She liked this. She liked lying naked and vulnerable on Keith's lap, blindfolded and at his mercy.

Something was happening to her spine. She was lying still, not moving, but it felt like she was almost . . . undulating.

Surrendering.

"You have a beautiful ass, Sarah."

Then he lifted his hand and brought it down on her bottom with an audible crack.

She gasped, but more from surprise than pain. It stung—no question about that—but it didn't really hurt. Still, as adrenaline coursed through her body, instinct made her squirm away from him.

Instantly he caught her wrists and bound them together behind her back, using something that felt like the tie of a robe. He must have had it ready.

Oh, God. What was wrong with her that she felt so excited right now? In a burst of clarity she realized that, on some level, she'd been telling herself this side of Keith was something she was putting up with in order to be with him. Like it was a flaw she had to accept.

But the truth was, she wanted this as much as he did. She loved everything they'd done together so far, and she wanted more.

"You're not going anywhere," he said in the low, sexy voice she adored.

When she struggled this time it wasn't instinct—it was because she wanted to. She wanted to feel how hopeless it was, how completely Keith could dominate her.

He held her down easily with a hand on her lower back.

"You were doing so well," he said, using his other hand to stroke her bare bottom again. The soft caress made her skin tighten everywhere, as though it were too small for her body. "And then you had to try and take your blindfold off. You should know better, Sarah. I make the rules at night."

Was he going to spank her again? She held her breath in anticipation, but he just kept stroking her.

"If you're a good girl, we won't have to do this again—even if your ass does look fucking amazing with the mark of my hand on it. But I'm willing to move on if you've learned your lesson. Have you?"

He was letting her off the hook. With one spank, he was letting her off the hook.

He thought she couldn't take it. He thought she didn't really like this. He'd talked about how rough he could be, and now he was backing off.

"No."

Keith's hand went still. "What?"

Her heart was pounding. "I said no. I haven't learned my lesson. I think . . ." She swallowed. "I think you should make sure I have."

The silence was so electric it seemed to crackle across her skin.

Then she felt his erection. The heat and hardness seemed to burn through his jeans. She remembered holding all that masculine power in her hands and her mouth last night, and a shiver went through her.

Keith's hand drifted slowly over her ass, paused, and then moved down between her legs. She wanted to part them further, but she couldn't seem to move. When he found the wetness there his hand went still again.

"Sarah," he said, his voice shaken.

There was no warning before the next spanking. This one was a little harder, but there was so much more pleasure than pain.

"Apparently you're a much naughtier girl than I realized. I think you need a lesson in which one of us has the upper hand."

When he said the word *hand* his came down again. The sting was like an electric shock, and she jumped and wriggled in his lap, feeling a pulse of excitement when she rubbed against the bulge in his jeans.

His hand came down again and again, raining sharp blows on her burning skin until it was almost too much.

Just before it was too much, he stopped. "Who's in charge here, Sarah?"

"You are," she gasped, and a delicious feeling swept through her when she said the words. Her ass was on fire and the burn spread all through her.

He untied her hands and shifted her off his lap, laying her on her back and reaching for her wrists. In seconds she was cuffed to the bed, the hot, tender skin of her backside rubbing against the silk comforter.

Keith slid one hand underneath to palm her bottom and laid the other across her damp pussy. The part of her that ached and throbbed was trapped between those strong hands, and even though she tried to stay still she twitched spasmodically in near-frantic desire.

Keith chuckled as he bent close to whisper in her ear. "Who's the master here?"

"You are."

The hand on her bottom moved so he could dip one finger into her honeyed wetness. Then she felt that slick finger at her anus.

She tensed up, and he chuckled again. "I think you want me everywhere, Sarah. I think you'll let me go anywhere I want to."

The hand on her pussy shifted, and she felt two fingers probing at her entrance, not penetrating yet but poised to do just that.

If she moved as much as a millimeter, he'd be inside her. She held herself still.

Then her breath whooshed out of her in a gasp as the finger at her anus pushed inside to the first knuckle.

She arched off the bed, and the movement thrust her onto the fingers at her pussy. When she tried to retreat from that invasion she impaled herself further on the finger in her ass.

The more she tried to get away the more she was invaded.

"Keith!"

As soon as she cried out his name she remembered that she was supposed to call him Sir, but he didn't say anything about it. A sound came from him, something between a groan and a growl.

"Take it deeper."

Oh, God. His words drove her over the edge and in the next instant she was rocking against him, shamelessly fucking his fingers on both ends. The friction inside her made her burn until every inch of her was on fire.

Then, suddenly, his fingers were gone. She opened her mouth to cry out in protest, but then she heard his zipper and the sound of foil ripping.

Her heart slammed against her chest. *Please, please, please, please...*

He shoved her legs roughly apart and gripped her hips.

"You're mine," he said, and pleasure exploded inside her as he drove his cock inside her, to the hilt.

He was so much bigger than the other guy she'd been with. He was so big she felt split in two. How could she contain so much?

When he started to move, it wasn't like his fingers. This was a true invasion. He was so long and thick it hurt just a little.

She wanted to hurt like this for the rest of her life. She wanted Keith inside her, possessing her, filling all her empty places. She wanted the friction, the heat and hardness, the big hands moving to her thighs, forcing her legs wider apart as he pushed inside her again and again.

She wanted those dominating thrusts telling her who she belonged to.

You're mine.

She was helpless under the onslaught. Her wrists were cuffed. Her legs were pinioned under his hands, her legs spread wide as he fucked her relentlessly, deliberately, thoroughly.

Then his angle shifted, and he was bumping against her clit with every flex of his hips. There was a roaring in her ears as the tension built to dizzying heights, her body like an elastic that had been pulled too tight.

And then she broke.

She was splintered by ecstasy, every cell in her body separately exploding.

Keith stayed deep inside her during her orgasm, grinding himself against her until the aftershocks rose suddenly into a second climax.

Her body was buzzing and quivering when he pulled out and slammed into her again, his thrusts harder and rougher than before. He pounded her mercilessly until she felt his cock pulse inside her, and then he called out her name as he shuddered with his own orgasm.

His weight collapsed on top of her, and for the first time she wished her hands weren't cuffed. She wanted to stroke his back, his shoulders, his hair.

Instead she lay still and basked in the feeling of his big body pinning hers to the mattress. He rested his head on her shoulder, and she let herself enjoy that, too.

"Sarah," he said after what seemed like a long, long time.

"Yes?" she whispered.

He shifted his head and pressed a kiss to her collarbone. "There's a possibility that you and I are sexually compatible."

A bubble of warmth and laughter rose inside her.

"Could be," she said gravely, wishing she could see his face but not asking this time.

They lay in silence for a while after that—a remarkably companionable silence.

It occurred to her that she couldn't remember ever feeling this relaxed with another human being.

Apparently the trick was to be tied down, blindfolded, and fucked senseless.

Another bubble of laughter rose, taking shape in a smile.

Keith finally eased himself to the side. "I'm sorry—I must have been heavy," he said, trailing a hand down her body from her neck to her waist.

"I liked it," she said simply, and then gasped when his hand covered her mound.

"Just staking out my territory," he said softly.

"You can't start anything now. My bones are already melted."

"I'm not starting anything," he said, the hint of a smile in his voice. "I just want to touch you."

"Well, I am in handcuffs. You can pretty much do anything you want."

"I like the sound of that."

His hand moved lazily upwards, across her belly to her breasts. He cupped one and leaned over to kiss the other.

"You have the most perfect breasts I've ever seen."

She couldn't let that pass—not when she thought about the women he must have been with over the years. "Oh, please."

"You don't believe me?"

"I most certainly do not."

He shifted so his hands covered both breasts, and her nipples pebbled into diamonds.

He pinched them hard. "Who's the master here?"

"You are," she gasped.

He pinched tighter. "Who has the most perfect breasts I've ever seen?"

"I do!"

"That's my girl," he said, and let her go.

My girl.

She bit her lip, telling herself not to hope.

But it wasn't possible. Despite all her efforts, hope took up residence in her heart.

Was there a chance that they could have more than this week? Or were the boundaries he'd drawn for them too thick?

She opened her mouth to speak and then closed it again. She couldn't have this conversation with a blindfold on.

She wasn't sure she could have this conversation at all.

But as though Keith had sensed her unspoken words, he reached up to release her cuffs.

The spell between them was broken.

"You can take off the blindfold after I'm gone."

And a minute later, he was.

CHAPTER 5

He'd managed to make it into the office today, but he'd skipped all his meetings. Now he was sitting at his desk with his head in his hands.

He was going to call off their deal. But he couldn't tell Sarah the real reason. He'd say he had to go out of the country, but since she'd honored her side of the bargain, the painting would still be hers.

The memory of last night flashed into his mind again, and he groaned.

The real reason he had to end it was that it mattered too much.

She mattered too much. And it was starting to mess with his head.

He looked up, and his eyes fell on the reproduction of *Nighthawks*.

The painting had been done in 1942. It showed a diner late at night with three customers, a man sitting on his own and a couple sitting together. The guy behind the counter was talking to the couple.

Sarah had asked him why that painting was his favorite, and he hadn't answered her.

He'd seen the painting for the first time when he was eleven or twelve, and even back then he'd identified with the man sitting on his own. He didn't look unhappy or lonely, or anything like that. He looked cool and solitary and complete within himself.

He looked content.

Now his eyes moved to the couple. They looked relaxed and easy, like they'd been together a long time.

They looked happy.

For the first time, he wondered what it would be like to identify with the man in the couple instead of the man sitting alone.

At two o'clock in the afternoon, Valerie knocked on the door. Without waiting for an invitation to enter, she came in with a big brown box in her arms.

"A messenger just dropped this off for you," she said.

He frowned at her. She was grinning, which was never a good sign. "Yeah? What is it?"

In answer she set the box down on the floor, and jumping, cavorting, galumphing out of it came a Jack Russell terrier.

His jaw dropped.

He knew immediately who'd done this. There was only one person in the entire world who would have done this.

Sarah Harper had gotten him a puppy.

He couldn't move. He just sat there, staring, as the puppy explored the office with over-the-top enthusiasm, discovering his existence after a few minutes with a frenzy of delight.

The puppy was too small to jump up on his lap, but that didn't stop him from trying.

After about thirty seconds of sitting there, frozen, while the small bundle of fur scrabbled at his pants and made eager, frantic puppy sounds, he gave in. He reached down and picked him up, holding him close enough to be slathered in sloppy kisses.

"My God," Valerie said in hushed tones. "Who are you, and what have you done with my boss?"

"I can't believe she did this," he murmured, setting the squirming puppy back down on the floor.

"Who?"

"Sarah Harper."

Valerie stared at him. "The one in the portrait?"

"Yeah. I knew her in high school and we . . . uh . . . reconnected this week."

Valerie raised her eyebrows. "I see."

She was eloquently silent after that, and Keith frowned at her.

"Wipe that grin off your face."

"I will not."

He looked away from her to watch the Jack Russell tear around the room. After a minute he paused to water a potted plant in the corner before charging off to attack a wastebasket.

"Did you see that? He peed in my office. That little monster just peed in my office."

He realized he was grinning, too, when he met Valerie's eyes again.

"I'll alert the cleaning company," she said. "So why did Sarah Harper get you a puppy?"

A tide of warmth rose up in him. "She wanted to make me happy."

"And did she?"

He couldn't seem to stop smiling. "Yeah, she did." He paused for a moment. "She does."

* * *

Sarah was sitting at her favorite desk in the library. Her computer was open in front of her, but she wasn't working. She was staring into space and thinking about Keith.

The messenger service had confirmed they had delivered the puppy an hour ago, but she hadn't heard from him.

She'd obviously made a mistake.

If he didn't want the dog, she would take him. Her landlord allowed pets.

If he didn't want her, that would be harder. But she'd just have to accept it.

And she did have a few more days with him . . . unless she'd messed everything up by going too far. Getting too personal. Breaking the rules.

She heard the library door opening, and she turned to see if Nancy was coming in.

But it wasn't Nancy. It was Keith. He stood in the doorway staring at her, and her body went hot all over, just like that day at the museum.

She hadn't seen him since the night they had dinner. She'd been blindfolded during every encounter with him. She'd heard his voice, she'd felt his touch, but she hadn't seen his face.

It felt shocking to see it now. To see him, and to see him looking at her. Somehow, she felt more naked than she had in his arms last night.

"You got me a puppy," he said after a moment.

She nodded slowly. "I did."

"If I'd wanted a puppy, I could have gotten one myself."

Her heart was pounding. "Sometimes people need a push."

His blue eyes lasered into hers. "Maybe they do." There was a short silence, and then he went on. "A puppy requires a lot of attention."

"Yes."

"What'll happen when I'm out of the country on business?"

"Um . . . Nancy?"

"I don't want to put more work on Nancy's plate."

She tilted her head to the side. "Rumor has it you're fairly well off. I bet you could hire someone to look after your dog while you're on business trips."

"You can't hire affection, which is what puppies need. I can't pay someone to love him the way I do."

Her heart turned over. "You love that puppy? But you just met him."

"I know it's soon. But that's what's in my heart." He took a step towards her. "I was hoping maybe you would help me out. We could share custody."

Her breath caught in her chest, and it was a minute before she could speak. "That would mean staying in each other's lives. Even after the week is over."

He nodded, his eyes never leaving hers. "That's what I want. If it's something you want."

She swallowed. "It is."

He took another step towards her. "Maybe you should think about it first. You'd be taking on a lot, Sarah. The puppy isn't house trained yet—and neither am I."

She smiled at him. "It won't be hard to train the puppy. Jack Russells are smart. As for you . . ." She paused. "I wouldn't change a thing. I like you exactly the way you are."

His eyes lit up, and she saw him take a deep breath. Then he crossed the room in a few long strides and took her in his arms, bending her back in a kiss that took her breath away.

When he finally broke away she was gasping.

"You're so beautiful," he whispered, framing her face in his hands and gazing at her. "It was torture staring at that portrait every day at the museum, knowing I'd never have the real thing. A part of me still can't believe this is real. That you're here, with me. Wanting to be with me."

"I want you to keep the portrait."

That took him aback. "But it's yours. I mean . . . it should be yours."

She shook her head. "I don't need it. I wanted it because it reminded me of my father, and because it gave me the illusion that we were connected."

She took a breath. "I loved my father, but we weren't connected. That takes work . . . and courage. My father and I had neither."

"But that painting . . ."

"It was always easy for my father to see people through his art. I think he did see me when he painted that portrait, and I'm grateful we had that, at least. But I'm looking for a different kind of connection now. The kind that's not at a safe distance."

His eyes searched hers. "What kind of connection are you looking for?"

"Something messy and human and scary. Something real."

He slid his arms around her waist. "I think I can offer you that."

"Good."

"I just want to be sure you understand . . ."

"What?"

"What I like in the bedroom—it's a part of who I am. That's not going to change."

"God, I hope not."

He took a step back and smiled at her. "You mean that?"

"Hell, yes."

"Then take off your clothes."

He was still smiling at her, but a wicked gleam had come into his eyes.

Goose bumps swept across her skin. "It's, um, daytime."

"Yes."

"Nancy could walk in, or Paul—"

"I sent them home. We're alone in the house."

She took a deep breath and let it out. She'd thought from the beginning that her being blindfolded had made Keith feel safe, and it probably had. But it had made her feel safe, too.

She couldn't move.

"Scared?" he asked softly.

She nodded.

"Too bad." He took another step back and folded his arms. "Do it now."

A shiver went through her, but she knew Keith wasn't kidding. When it came to sex, he gave the orders. She could follow them or go home.

Her choice.

She reached for the hem of her tee shirt and pulled it up over her head. Then she reached behind her for the clasp on her bra and undid it, letting it fall to the ground.

"Nice," Keith said, moving close enough that he could cover her breasts with his hands. Her hardening nipples poked into his palms.

"Lose the pants," he instructed, and she kicked off her sandals before tugging her jeans and panties down.

In a few seconds she stood naked in front of Keith Logan.

"Even nicer," he said, and she could see the desire in his eyes—the expression she'd only imagined before. "Now go to the desk and bend over."

A flutter of excitement made her knees weak, but she made it to the desk without collapsing. Then she rested her forearms on the table as she bent at the waist.

"Spread your legs wider," he said, and as she did she heard the sound of his zipper.

She bit her lip as moisture flooded her core. Then Keith put one hand on her hip and used the other to stroke her.

"You're wet," he murmured, and then he landed a sharp spank on her bottom.

Adrenaline spiked in her bloodstream, and now she was even wetter.

"Do you want me?" he asked roughly, and she started to say yes. But then she shook her head. "No."

His hands tightened on her and she knew her answer had surprised and excited him.

"I think you're lying, Sarah. You've been thinking about me all day, haven't you? Thinking about my cock inside you."

"No," she said again, and he spanked her twice more.

"It doesn't matter if you want me or not. I'm going to fuck you and there's nothing you can do about it."

Because she loved to feel his strength she used her hands to push against the desk, trying to straighten up.

But he was too fast for her. He caught her wrists and twisted them behind her back, and then he tied them with—what was that?

His belt. She didn't know why that was so sexy, but it was.

With her hands bound she was almost helpless. Still she kept struggling even when Keith held her down easily with one hand on her back, pressing her breasts against the cool wood of the desk.

Then she felt the tip of his cock against her sopping entrance.

"Do you want me?" he asked again, rougher than before.

"No!" she cried out, even as her body quivered with eagerness.

Then he pushed inside her, slow and deliberate, while he used the fingers of one hand to massage her clit.

She was trapped between his cock and his fingers, and she found herself pushing back and then forward, delicious sensation waiting for her everywhere. She moaned.

Keith bent over her and whispered in her ear. "You need this hard cock, don't you?"

Her role fell away and the truth slipped out. "Yes . . . oh, God, yes . . ."

He fucked her harder, deeper, and his fingers on her clit moved faster.

"You'll let me fuck you whenever I want to."

"Yes . . ."

"Tell me who you belong to."

"You!"

"That's my girl," he growled, and then he was pounding her so hard and fast she couldn't form a thought, much less a word—except for his name.

"Keith!" she cried out, climaxing in a fevered rush as her muscles clamped around him, milking his cock until he came, too.

The only sound in the room was the ragged gasp of their breath and the pounding of their hearts.

After the hurricane in her body died down she became aware that Keith was nuzzling the back of her neck. She arched into him, and he undid the belt around her wrists. Then he pulled her upright and spun her so they were face to face.

He slid his hands into her hair and kissed her, and she wrapped her arms around him as she kissed him back with everything in her heart—even the things she hadn't said yet.

She didn't feel in a rush to speak the words. When the time was right, she wouldn't be able to hold them back.

The kiss ended, and she pulled back to look at him. He was smiling, and something in his eyes told her he already knew what she was still too shy to say.

ABOUT THE AUTHOR

Kate Grey believes that a good love story should make you sigh and a good love scene should make you squirm—in the best possible way. Her dream is to find the perfect balance between romantic and sexy, and since she's fairly certain she'll never reach that goal, she's probably going to be writing for a long, long time. She's currently at work on her fourth book.

She loves to hear from readers and can be reached at kategreywrites@gmail.com.

Books by Kate Grey

By His Desire
His One Desire
Only Desire

Printed in Great Britain
by Amazon.co.uk, Ltd.,
Marston Gate.